BE A FRIEND

SALINA YOON

BLOOMSBURY

LONDON OXFORD NEW YORK NEW DELHI SYDNEY

FOR BEN AND SAMMI

Bloomsbury Publishing, London, Oxford, New York, New Delhi and Sydney

First published in the United States of America in 2016
by Bloomsbury Children's Books
1385 Broadway, New York, New York 10018

This edition first published in Great Britain in 2016 by Bloomsbury Publishing Plc
50 Bedford Square, London WC1B 3DP

BLOOMSBURY is a registered trademark of Bloomsbury Publishing Plc

Text and illustrations copyright © Salina Yoon 2016
The moral rights of the author/illustrator have been asserted

A CIP catalogue record of this book is available from the British Library

ISBN 978 1 4088 6909 3

Printed in China by Leo Paper Products, Heshan, Guangdong

1 3 5 7 9 10 8 6 4 2

www.bloomsbury.com

BLOOMSBURY is a registered trademark of Bloomsbury Publishing Plc

DENNIS was an

ordinary boy . . .

. . . who expressed himself in **EXTRAORDINARY** ways.

Everyone called him
MIME BOY.

Dennis didn't speak a word.

He would only **ACT** – in scenes.

Some children would **SHOW** and
TELL in class.

Dennis would **MIME** instead.

EGG

CATERPILLAR

CHRYSALIS

BUTTERFLY

Some children liked to **CLIMB** a tree.

Dennis was happy to **BE** a tree.

But even trees get **LONELY** sometimes.

Dennis felt **INVISIBLE**.

It was as if he were standing on the other side of a **WALL**.

Until . . .

One day Dennis kicked an **IMAGINARY** ball . . .

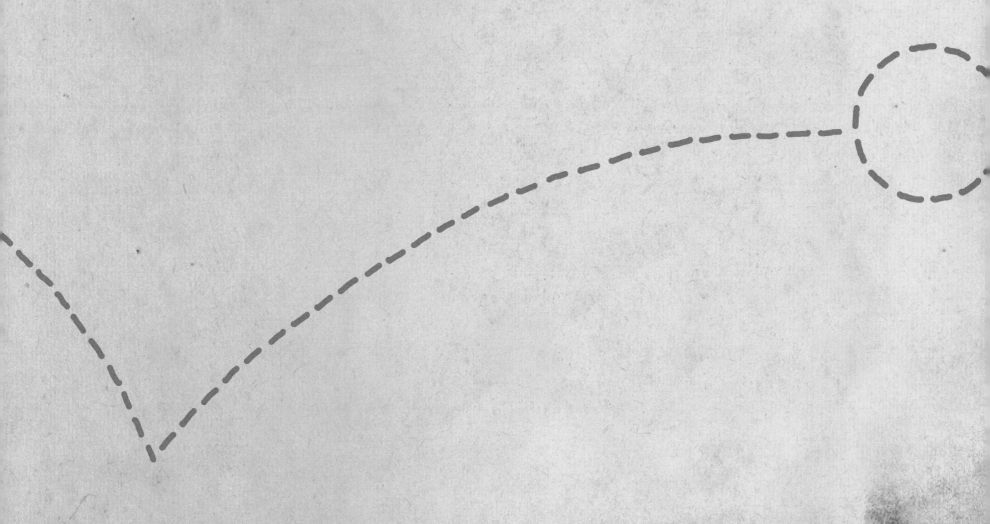

. . . and someone **CAUGHT** it!

Her name was **JOY**.

There was no

wall between

Dennis and Joy.

It was more
like a **MIRROR**.

They saw the world the **SAME** way.

Dennis and Joy didn't speak a **WORD**,

because **FRIENDS** don't have to.

But they laughed out loud with
JAZZ HANDS . . .

. . . for all the world to **SEE!**